A Rainy Day Story

KAR-BEN PUBLISHING®
An imprint of Lerner Publishing Group, Inc.,
241 First Avenue North
Minneapolis, MN 55401 USA

Website address: www.karben.com

Main body text set in Avenir
Typeface provided by Adobe Systems

Library of Congress Cataloging-in-Publication Data

The Cataloging-in-Publication Data for *A Rainy Day Story* is on file at the
   Library of Congress.
ISBN 978-1-5415-6038-3 (lib. bdg.)
ISBN 978-1-5415-6039-0 (pbk.)

PJ Library Edition ISBN 978-1-72842-025-7

Manufactured in China
1-49133-49293-2/28/2020

092035.1K1/B1533/A6

A Rainy Day Story

by Ruth Calderon

illustrated by Noa Kelner

KAR-BEN
PUBLISHING

One day, Rabbi Hanina Ben Dosa was walking along when it started to rain.

Raindrops fell on his nose,
on his cheeks,
and on his ears.
His hair was wet,
and water dripped down his forehead
and into his eyes.

His collar was drenched,
and raindrops rolled down his back.

His legs were wet.
Rabbi Hanina
was soaked to the bone!

Rabbi Hanina looked around.
The trees were rinsing off their dusty leaves,
the soil was soaking up the raindrops,
flowers were holding their heads up high,
and frogs were jumping in the puddles.

Rabbi Hanina looked to the heavens and said,
"Master of the Universe!
The whole world is happy,
and Hanina is suffering?
My clothes are soaked,
my body is shivering,
and my sandals are covered in mud.
I'm so cold!"

The rain stopped.

Rabbi Hanina returned home, soaking wet.

He took off his muddy sandals

and put them next to the oven.

He peeled off his wet clothes.

Rabbi Hanina put on a dry cloak.

A pot of soup was cooking in the kitchen,
a fire was burning in the stove,
and he was warm and comfortable.

The soup was ready,

but Rabbi Hanina didn't sit down to eat it.

He walked over to the window and looked outside.

The ground was parched,

the trees were thirsty,

the river was dry,

and the frogs were staring at the sky longingly.

How could this be?

The rain had stopped, and
Rabbi Hanina was warm and comfortable.

But what about the rest of the world?

Rabbi Hanina looked to the heavens and said,

"Master of the Universe!

The whole world is suffering,

and Hanina is happy?"

All of a sudden,
lightning flashed,

thunder rumbled,

and rain poured down.

Rabbi Hanina smiled to himself.
He sat at the table,
filled his hungry belly with the tasty soup,
and breathed in the sweet smell of the rain.

ר' חנינא בן דוסא הוה קא אזיל באורחא

אתא מיטרא

אמר לפניו רבונו של עולם כל העולם כולו בנחת וחנינא בצער

פסק מיטרא

כי מטא לביתיה אמר לפניו רבונו של עולם כל העולם כולו בצער וחנינא בנחת

אתא מיטרא

Rabbi Hanina is walking along a road when it begins to rain. "Master of the Universe," he says to God. "The entire world is comfortable because they needed rain, but I am getting wet and suffering." Rabbi Hanina gets home and the rain stops. "Master of the Universe," he says to God. "The entire world is suffering because the rain has stopped, so how is it right that I am comfortable?" And the rain starts again.

—*Babylonian Talmud, Taanit 24b*

About the Author

RUTH CALDERON is the Caroline Zelaznik Gruss and Joseph S. Gruss Visiting Professor in Talmudic civil law at Harvard Law School. A former member of Knesset, she is also an educator and academic Talmud scholar. She is the founder of the Elul pluralistic beit midrash, as well as Alma, the Home for Hebrew Culture. She received her MA and PhD in Talmud from the Hebrew University. This is her first children's book. The mother of Miriam, Naomi and Shaul, she lives in Tel Aviv, Israel.

About the Illustrator

NOA KELNER graduated from the Bezalel Academy of Art and Design. Her illustrations have appeared in books, newspapers, and magazines. She teaches illustration and is the cofounder and artistic director of the annual Outline—Illustration and Words festival in Jerusalem. She lives in Israel with her husband and two children.